The Ugly Duckling

Illustrated by Dorothea King

GONDOLA

Mother Duck had five broken egg
shells, and five new ducklings.
She had one egg which did not
have a crack in it.
"I wonder when that egg
will hatch," said Mother Duck.
All of the animals that lived
in the farmyard came to look
at the egg.
"That is too big to be
a duck's egg," said a chicken.

"That will hatch into a turkey,"
said a goose.
"How will I know if it is
a turkey?" asked Mother Duck.
"It will not swim," said
the goose.
At last the egg hatched. The bird
which stepped from the broken
shell did not look like his
brothers and sisters at all.
But he was not a turkey
for he went down to the pond
and began to swim.

"What an ugly little duckling
you are," laughed the chickens.
"What an ugly little duckling
you are," laughed the geese.
"What an ugly little duckling
you are," laughed all
the other ducks.

The little duckling was so
unhappy. He had no friends.
EVERYONE laughed at him,
even his mother.
He decided to run away.
"Nobody will miss me," he said.
And nobody did.

He made his home on the marshes.
One day he saw some wild ducks
swimming in a lake.
"Will you be my friends?" he asked.
"What an ugly little duckling you
are," laughed the wild ducks.
"We do not want you on our lake."
They chased him away.

One day the little duckling saw
some swans flying across the sky.
"I wish I were a swan," he said.
"Swans are beautiful. Nobody
laughs at them." He felt sadder
than ever as he watched
them fly away.

Winter came. The days were cold. The nights were even colder. Food was very hard to find. Now the little duckling was not only lonely, he was cold and hungry too. One cold night the lake froze. When morning came the duckling's feet were stuck firmly in the ice. He could not move. "Now I will die," he said.

A farmer was taking his dog for a walk. He saw the duckling stuck in the ice.
"We must get you out of there," said the farmer. He broke the ice with a stick. "Go and find your friends," he said.
"I wish I had friends to find," said the little duckling sadly.

Spring came at last. The days
grew warmer. There was plenty
to eat. The wild ducks and geese
came back to the lake. They had
all been away for the winter.
They splashed about in the water
and they all talked at once.
They had so much to tell one
another. But nobody spoke
to the little duckling.
"I wish they would talk to me,"
he said.

Sadly, the little duckling spread his wings and flew up into the clear blue sky. He had never flown before and he was surprised how strong his wings were.
He should have been happy, but he was not. He looked down at the ground far below him. He could see swans swimming in a pond in a beautiful garden. He would ask them to help him.

He flew down to the pond and
settled on the water.
He called to the swans.
"Please come and kill me.
I am so ugly, and I am
so lonely I do not want to live."
"Ugly? You?" said the swans
looking surprised. "Have you
looked at yourself in the pond?"

The little duckling looked down
into the water. Looking back
at him was a swan.
"Is . . . is that me?" he asked.
"But I am beautiful."
"Of course you are," said the
swans. "You are a swan. All swans
are beautiful."

Three children came running
to the pond.
"Look!" they cried. "A new swan.
Please stay in our pond. We will
come and see you every day."
The little duckling had changed
into a beautiful swan during the
long cold winter. He would never
be lonely again.